The Pattersons at Turkey Hill House

THE PATTERSONS AT TURKEY HILL HOUSE

BROADMAN PRESS
Nashville, Tennessee

4248-01
ISBN: 0–8054–4801–2

Library of Congress Catalog Card Number: 79–52002
Dewey Decimal Classification: F

Printed in the United States of America

TO
MY CHILDREN
WILLIAM AND JULIE

The Pattersons at Turkey Hill House

1

Frank Patterson moved to another blackberry bush. That wasn't easy to do, for the briars were thick. And where there weren't briars there were weeds and little pine trees. Several times he had to pick a long, cruel briar away from his shirt or pants.

Frank was twelve, a big boy for his age. He was husky, his mother said, but his friends in Atlanta called him fat. He didn't like that anymore than he liked his curly hair. He wished his hair were straight. But the Pattersons all had curly hair except for Mama. Hers was straight and long.

"I don't like picking blackberries," cried Shelley, Frank's littlest sister, who was not quite six years old. "The bushes are too sticky!" She had curly brown hair that was like a furry cap around her round, rosy face.

"But we have to get enough for a pie. You know that's how I talked Mama into letting us come, Shelley. I told her that we'd get some berries for a pie."

"Well, they're not very good. I bet Daddy won't even like the pie."

"Oh, Shelley, don't be such a baby!" exclaimed David Oliver. "You've probably been eating red berries. You'll get a stomachache and Mama'll never let us go adventuring again." He threw a berry in his pan and it made a loud "ping" on the empty bottom.

David Oliver wasn't fat like Frank, but his ears stuck out. He didn't really care. He was eight years old and what he cared about was having fun.

"Well, I don't care if she doesn't let us come again!" declared Shelley. "This adventure isn't very nice!"

"Shelley, why don't you just sit down in this little patch of weeds until we get through," said Rita, who at ten was a very motherly little girl. She was trying to let her hair grow out and it was getting bushy. She had pretty little soft brown freckles across her nose, too.

Shelley agreed to sit down and rest in the weed patch. But she was not very happy. The summer sun was hot with no big trees for shade. The weeds were itchy, and there were big, green insects that she'd never seen before. Rita said they were June bugs. June bugs had never come to their yard in Atlanta. But here at Aunt Minnie's house in Stanton there were all kinds of things.

The four children had been so excited about coming to live in Aunt Minnie's house for the summer. Just the name, Turkey Hill House, made it interesting to them. In fact, they had wanted to move for good. And so had Daddy. He wanted to be a country doctor instead of a city doctor. But Mama didn't want to. She had finally agreed to come just for the summer.

Of course that meant that Daddy had to keep working in Atlanta. But he came up on weekends. He would be coming tonight, and Mama was going to surprise him with a pie if they could get enough berries.

From where they were picking, the children could just see the roof of Turkey Hill House with its two brick chimneys, one at each end. Frank and Rita could remember visiting Aunt Minnie there several times. Now she had died and willed the whole place to Daddy. The woods and everything.

Frank stopped picking for a minute and shaded his eyes as he looked up at the hill behind Turkey Hill House. The woods started at the edge of a grassy slope, a dark exciting woods. He wanted so much to explore them, but so far Mama had said no. She was afraid of things, anything that moved. But maybe soon they could go. He walked toward a loaded bush.

"How many berries do you have, David Oliver?" asked Rita.

"Not many. And I'm getting tired. When we going to quit?"

"When we get enough berries."

"Well, gosh, Rita, look how many you have. She could make a pie just from yours."

All this time Shelley had been sitting quietly

in the spot Rita had found for her. She had twisted
two tall grasses together to make a chain. But she
couldn't get them to tie around her neck. Then
she saw some pretty blue flowers near an old
broken fence where the pasture used to be. She
waded through the weeds and carefully pulled
briars apart to get to them.

David Oliver decided to rest and count his
berries, much to Frank's disgust. Frank was still
trying to fill the pan his mother had given him.
He was leaning into a clump of briars where there
were lots of blackberries and had just picked a
handful when he heard Shelley screaming. He
turned to look.

Shelley was standing almost hidden by briars
and brush. She was standing stiff as a statue with

her hands held tightly together. Her little round face was full of terror as she screamed.

Frank and Rita both hurried to her, spilling their own berries. As Frank got close there was a rustle near his feet. Looking down he saw a brown snake slither out of sight under the bushes.

"Did the snake scare you, Shelley?" he asked, trying to pick the little girl up. She was still standing just the same, only now she had both hands to her face, hanging onto it as if it might come off.

"Please, Shelley, hush screaming. Mama will hear you," said Rita, trying to hug her.

Just then Frank noticed something red on Shelley's white sock. At first he thought it was berry juice. Then he knew it was blood. Terror filled his heart. The snake! Shelley was snakebitten!

"We've got to get her out of here," he yelled and he picked her up, stiff as she was, and went crashing through the bushes to the open field. Then he started up toward the two-story house on the hill. It looked like such a long way to the shade of the big oak tree by the corner of the porch.

Mrs. Patterson was defrosting the refrigerator. It was a very old one, and she was humming as she wiped the rusty shelves. Fridays were so good because John came home on Fridays. He would really be surprised to have a blackberry cobbler since he didn't know she could make it. She smiled to herself.

She had just gotten down on her knees to clean the vent at the bottom of the refrigerator when she thought she heard a scream. She held her breath. It was a scream! She jumped up and ran to the back porch. The screaming was coming from the blackberry patch.

For a minute her feet just wouldn't move. She was afraid to find out what was wrong. But she had to. Finally she took a deep breath and ran down the six steps. Then she saw Frank way down the hill, struggling to carry Shelley. She ran to meet him, her heart sounding like thunder in her ears.

"Shelley! Frank! What's wrong?" she cried, taking Shelley into her arms.

"She's been bitten, Mama," said Rita, her voice shaking.

"Bitten! By what?"

"A snake, Mama."

"Are you sure? Oh, my baby!" she said as she started back to the house.

The emergency room at the small county hospital was full of people. But the only doctor was in surgery. The nurses were doing the best they could to take care of everybody. One of them took Shelley and laid her in a little room on a steel table.

Frank, Rita, and David Oliver could hear their mother and the nurse trying to calm Shelley down.

"I wish we'd never gone berry picking," said Frank.

"Me, too," said Rita, crying softly.

David Oliver walked over to the door where Shelley's screams were still so loud. He walked back and forth. Hospitals were so boring. There was nothing to do.

A man with a paper started reading: "FBI agents are searching for a convict who escaped this morning from a reform school in North Georgia. He is not armed as far as officials know."

Frank was only half-listening because of Shelley's screams. But suddenly the screams stopped. The man stopped reading. Everyone looked startled. Frank and Rita looked at each other in terror. Why would Shelley have stopped screaming—unless she were dead?

The door opened. Mrs. Patterson came out looking very white. It made her long dark hair look even darker.

"The nurse says it's not a snakebite," she said, and smiled weakly. "Those marks are just briar scratches."

Frank put his hands over his face and leaned his elbows on his knees.

"Frank, she'll be OK," said Mrs. Patterson, putting an arm across his shoulders. "Don't worry. We finally got a shot in her and it's calmed her down."

"Oh, Mom, I thought she was dead!" cried Frank. "And it would have been my fault for not taking better care!"

"It wouldn't have been your fault! Anyway, she's

fine. I do want the doctor to see her, though. If he would only come," she said, looking up and down the hallways anxiously.

"We all want the doctor to come, lady," said the man with the paper. "A town with one doctor is pretty bad off. That's what I say." His wife punched him and he groaned and went back to reading the paper.

It was two hours before Dr. Guy checked Shelley. By then she was feeling fine. He gave Mrs. Patterson some medicine to help Shelley rest that night if she had trouble. She had been so terribly frightened.

It was dark when they got back to Turkey Hill House, the big house with a porch around three sides, the house with the many tall windows. Frank remembered suddenly about the convict who had escaped that day and shivered as his mother unlocked the door. But light soon filled the house and no one thrust a gun at them from behind a door.

"It's all Shelley's fault we don't have a blackberry pie," grumbled David Oliver.

2

Shelley was slow in getting over her fright. Frank and David Oliver made some insect cages one day with some old pieces of screen they had found. Shelley wouldn't come out on the porch to see the insect race between two Georgia thumpers—big colorful, muscular grasshoppers.

Mrs. Rath came and brought a neighbor lady to see Mama. Rita noticed that the lady smelled like fresh doughnuts and, judging by her large stomach, decided she was a good cook like Mrs. Rath. As the children played with the insects, the ladies sat around the big round kitchen table talking about flowers, recipes, and things. There were bees humming comfortably in a sweet smelling bush nearby.

"Have you heard about the Dickerson boy?" asked the lady named Mrs. Hill.

"Dickerson?" asked Mrs. Rath.

"You know, his dad's a lawyer. They moved here last year from North Carolina. They live on the other side of Stanton in that brick house that sits way up on an open hill. Just past the Frazier place. You know the one."

"Yes, I remember now. But what about the boy?"

"Well, something awful happened before they moved here. Something that made the boy withdraw. They say he'll hardly speak to his parents. I think it's been far worse than the usual problems between child and parent. Anyway," she said, drawing in her breath from talking so fast, "now he's run away."

"Oh, no, how terrible for all of them!" said Mrs. Rath, instantly concerned. "No trace?"

"No trace at all. Only a note, I heard. It said he had to fight his battle alone and they're afraid of what that may mean."

"Poor boy, what could he have done that was so awful?" Mrs. Patterson always felt a yearning to reunite families that were broken for any reason.

"I really don't know what happened," answered Mrs. Hill. "I've always had the feeling whenever I met that woman, though, that she was grieving about something. They've visited our church, but they don't seem to want anyone to speak to them. They always leave in a hurry."

"Speaking of church," said Mrs. Rath, changing the subject, "how about visiting with us Sunday, Martha?"

"Oh, I don't know. Our weekends with John are so short. But I do miss our church back home."

"Then you'll come?"

"Let's do, Mama!" exclaimed Shelley.

16

"Well . . . OK . . . we'd love to, Jane. Is it . . . ?"

"It's right down the road, a new brick building on the right. Bethel Baptist Church. You can't miss it."

"Oh, yes, I could," laughed Martha. "But John will be here; he can find anything."

When Sunday came, the Pattersons went to church. After going just one Sunday, Mrs. Patterson made so many new friends that almost every day someone was coming to share garden tips or a new recipe. Some of them came to get help on a handwork problem, for that was what Mrs. Patterson could share with them.

Frank sat on his windowsill one day, feeling the uncurtained breeze blowing on his warm, moist face. He could look down on the roof of the porch and then way out over the valley to the distant blue peaks of the mountains. It was too bad Aunt Minnie had to die, but, since she had, it was wonderful she had willed this house to Daddy.

A swelling of love for this place made him feel like doing something, flying like a bird, or swimming a river, or riding a horse across an open range. He closed his eyes and smelled the house— a mixture of musty mattresses, cracking paint, and a cake baking downstairs.

"Mama's happy now," he said to himself dreamily. "Maybe now would be a good time to ask if we can go to the woods."

They had gotten permission to go to Mrs. Rath's

store pretty freely. That seemed more city-like to his mother, he supposed. But any mention of the woods had brought an instant no. His mother was a very gentle woman until you were on opposite sides of a question. Then she didn't seem so gentle.

"I'm going to ask her anyway," he said to the mountains. "I'll do it right now."

It was a day they'd never forget, that first day in the woods. Mama had said not to go far. But she did let them go. All except Shelley. Shelley wanted to go but she was afraid. They promised to bring her something special from the woods.

Out of the sunlight and openness of the grassy hillside into the mysterious dark depths of the woods they went. "It's beautiful," Frank and Rita said at the same time.

"Where's the excitement?" questioned David Oliver, looking around in bewilderment.

Since they weren't to go far, they played around on the top of the hill for awhile. Frank found a tree from which he could look down on the top of the house one way and across a valley to another hilltop on the other side. It was an oak tree whose lower limbs stretched out far and suddenly dipped close to the ground. He had climbed one of the limbs. Across on the other hill was a really tall pair of pine trees. They stood far taller than the rest of the trees around them as if they were a king and his queen.

"Boy! I bet I could really see from one of those

trees," Frank said to himself and immediately had a new longing.

"Come down, come down," squealed Rita just then. "We've found a bird's nest. Oh, come, Frank, and see this little nest."

He wished for the thousandth time that he weren't fat as he climbed awkwardly down the limb. Daddy said he ought to leave off some desserts. That was hard to do!

The bird's nest was a tiny cave among the thick leaves under some low huckleberry bushes. There were three brown-speckled eggs in it.

"If I were a bird, that's the kind of nest I'd want," said Rita.

"I bet it's dangerous," commented David Oliver. "Just think of all the things that could eat you up."

"David Oliver . . ." began Rita, but Frank put his finger to his lips and looked significantly over her shoulder. Looking behind her, she saw a little brown bird, one wing drooping, hopping miserably along.

"Oh, the poor thing!" exclaimed Rita and she stood up to rescue the little bird. The others tried to help her corner the bird so she could catch it, but it was afraid of them and kept hopping away. Soon they found themselves down in the valley far from the nest. Right when they thought Frank was going to pick the bird up, it flew straight up to a limb way above them and began to chirp and fuss.

"That sorry bird was being dishonest," grumbled David Oliver, who had really thought they might put a splint on its wing.

Frank burst into laughter. "I bet she didn't want us looking at her nest. Wow! What a smart bird! Go on home, lady bird, we won't bother your little eggs," he called up to her. And, just as if she understood him, she flew back where they'd come from.

When they looked around, they saw that they weren't far from a wet weather spring and that not far beyond it, across a sandy, floor-washed area, was the next hill. Some mountain laurel had a few pink flowers left over from spring. A huge hollow tree stood just a few steps up the side of the steep hill.

"Wow!" said David Oliver. "We are really in the woods now. This *is* better than Atlanta."

"Yeah. Wish we could go on," said Frank. "I wonder if the brook's on the other side of that hill. There's supposed to be a brook somewhere on this place. Daddy said there was."

"Why can't we go on?" asked David Oliver. "Mama won't mind."

"Oh, yes, she will," said Frank. "We better go back now so she'll let us come again."

"Oh, Frank," said Rita, "do we have to?"

"We haven't anything special for Shelley yet," said David Oliver suddenly.

"Well, we can get something on the way back."

"What? An old feather or something?"

So finally Frank gave in. After all, it couldn't take long just to go look. They just wouldn't tell Mama how far they'd come.

The brook was in the next valley. At first they could only hear it, as the laurels were so thick around it. Then, as they got closer, they could see flashes of water through the bushes. Finally, parting the branches and shoving through the thick foliage, they stood beside the gushing stream. Right at that point there were big mossy stones jutting up out of the water, and the banks, too, were covered with soft moss.

Almost instantly their shoes were off and they were squealing about how cold the water was.

"This water must have come straight from Alaska," said David Oliver, climbing out to feel the warm furry moss under his feet.

They found beautiful stones in the water. Smooth, roundish ones, bright rusty red ones, bluish ones with almost mirror-like shiny flecks in them.

"These are what we can take to Shelley," said Frank, glad that they had finally come on.

"But what if Mama knows where they came from?" asked Rita.

"She won't. Remember, she doesn't know anything about the country."

"Well, Shelley sure will be proud . . . what is it, Frank?"

"Shush! I thought I heard someone walking," he whispered, wondering why he was suddenly so afraid. He realized how far they were from anyone and how the woods were heavy with some kind of mystery.

They were all quiet, but the only sounds were the water gushing over and around stones and a blue jay squealing from high in a tree. Frank was almost convinced he hadn't heard steps when suddenly a twig cracked not very far away. Heavy footsteps were rustling toward them through the bushes.

They grabbed their shoes up, dropping their pebbles inside them, and ran, hearts thudding, back the way they had come. Whoever it was, friend or foe, they didn't want to be seen. If it were a friend, he might tell Mama where he found them. If it were an enemy, no telling what would happen. Frank remembered the convict again. Surely he had been found by now.

3

Frank didn't hear anymore about the convict, but he and the other children played closer to home after their scare. But Frank kept wanting to go to the brook again.

"Well, Miss Priss," said Dad to Shelley one Sunday as they all sat around the big oak table in the kitchen. "you're going to have a birthday soon, I believe."

Shelley giggled happily and left her plate to climb upon Daddy's knee.

Dad was very young-looking with a well-trimmed, dark mustache to give him a distinguished look. The glasses helped, too, to make him look doctorly. Even so, people were always asking him how long till he would get his full degree, as if he were just an intern. They couldn't believe it when he laughed and told them he had a twelve-year-old son.

"Stuart's coming to my party, Daddy," said Shelley.

"Stuart?"

"He's my new boyfriend," she said and giggled behind her hand.

"He live out near the Dickersons," said Mrs. Patterson.

"Have you heard anymore about the runaway boy?" asked Dr. Patterson.

"Oh, yes, I did. Someone said that his mother died years ago and this Mrs. Dickerson is a stepmother. She and the boy got along just terribly it seems."

"Hmmmm. A sad case. I hope they find him soon."

"Where do you think he might go, Dad?" asked Frank.

"Probably California. That's where desperate kids seem to think they can find their answers. And listen to me, you kids of mine," he said, holding Shelley with one arm and using the other to point sternly at each one of them. "If you ever decide to run away, come tell me you're leaving first."

"Aw, Daddy," laughed Rita. "Then there wouldn't be any use!"

"Come on, children," said Mama briskly, "help me clean up the dishes. Then, if you promise you won't go far, you can go to the woods for a little while."

Before they went to the woods, Frank got four short boards, some nails, and a hammer out of the shed. Mama and Dad were on the front porch and didn't see him so he didn't have to try to explain what he was going to do with the things. To the children he just said he wanted to make something.

Shelley decided to go this time. She got tired before they even got to the second hill and they had to stop and rest with her. Finally they got to the top. The two tall pines were not so different from those around them when the children saw them up close. They had looked so much taller from a distance. But even up close they still looked kingly.

"Okay, Frank, what are you going to make?" asked David Oliver.

"I'm going to make a ladder on this tall pine. So we can climb way up and look out."

"Oh, boy!" squealed Rita with delight. "Hurry, Frank, and make it."

It was a wonderful idea even if it wasn't good for the tree. Now, by taking turns they could climb the nailed-on ladder up to the lowest limbs and climb higher to where they could see for miles around. They could even see the far distant ranges of mountains. Of course David Oliver and Shelley were too small to take the long stretchy steps, but Frank and Rita gave them detailed reports. After a while, David Oliver and Shelley got bored and started raking the leaves to form streets in a pretend village.

Frank was up in the tree, standing on a strong limb and looking across the second valley towards Stanton. Something suddenly caught his eye. He gripped the trunk of the tree tighter and looked to be sure it really was so. There was smoke, blue smoke, rising gently in a tiny spiral and hanging like a little cloud just above the trees in the valley. Someone had a fire down there. The same someone whom they had heard walking before? The convict?

Frank decided not to say anything about it, not even to Rita. Maybe she wouldn't notice. Mama would never let them come if she found out about it. "Say, Rita, let's go back down," he said as casually as he could and then when they were down he said to all of them, "Listen! Let's go build a fort dam in that gully toward home."

"Gee, that'd be fun!" cried David Oliver, enthusiastic about anything to do with an army.

They played until it was almost dusk down in

the valley, but when they climbed the hill and came out on the open grass, they were in sunshine again.

"Come on, race you!" said Rita, and Frank began to run, knowing full well that she would win. She always did.

Frank didn't mean to slip up on Mama and Dad. He was just out of breath and was heading silently for the front porch, having left the others getting water in the kitchen, when he heard the tone of their voices—the Deep Discussion Tone. He leaned against the door facing, feeling the coolness of the old wood against his hot face.

"Part of me does want to, John. Really. But I'm so scared. It gets so terribly quiet when everyone goes to sleep at night, and then I start hearing the most awful things creeping around outside."

"You just don't realize that they're mostly very kind sounds you hear," he said gently.

"I know that. But I don't feel it. My stomach ties up in knots thinking of all the things that the children can get into."

"But think what they can get into in the city. Think of the drug racket. Think of the muggers on the streets."

"I know, John. But, please, don't push me. I have done well, you'll have to admit. I've come a long way. I even let the children have an insect race on the porch one day, though I felt creepy and crawly for days afterward."

"I love you, Martha."

"I love you, too, John. And wherever that Dickerson boy is I wish he knew someone loves him, too."

"Whatever made you think of him right now?"

"Well, I don't know. You know, I didn't tell you all that I knew about the Dickerson boy because I hated for the children to hear. John, he shot his little sister, his new mother's little girl."

"Shot her? Did she die?"

"No. But she's paralyzed from the waist down. It was an accident, John, a terrible, terrible accident, but he can never forget it. He couldn't get along with Mrs. Dickerson, but he loved that little girl. Irene says the child loved him so much that the mother was jealous and refused to let her talk to Kevin after the accident."

"Such a mess of mixed-up emotions!"

"Isn't it though!"

Frank crept to the stairs and up to his room. He needed to sit in his window and think. Where would he go if he had shot dear little Shelley and caused her to be crippled? To California? To the redwood forest maybe? It did sound like a forgiving kind of place. He shuddered as he remembered how awful he'd felt when he thought Shelley might die from a snakebite.

4

Shelley's birthday party was a big success, even though Daddy wasn't there. They had it on Saturday afternoon thinking he would be there, but one of his patients had a heart attack and he didn't even come home at all that weekend. Mrs. Rath brought her ice cream freezer and some of the other mothers came and visited while the children played.

There were potato races. A child would put a potato between his knees and try to reach a goal before anyone else. There were sack races. Running or hopping in a big cloth feed sack was not easy, but somehow David Oliver won. And then there was a scavenger hunt. Each child was given a list of things to collect in a bag.

Frank enjoyed the party up to a point, even though the children were Shelley's age. But two hours was enough. He wished he could slip off to the woods all by himself, even without Rita. He had been afraid at first of the thought of meeting someone in the lonely woods. But maybe the stranger needed him. Maybe he was hurt. Or maybe he was just a lonesome, lost person. He pictured himself as a heroic rescuer of someone in trouble.

He surveyed the hillside and knew there was no way he could slip off that way without being noticed. But there was a little path that went around the hill to what used to be a pigpen. It was pretty grown up and jungly, but he thought he could manage to get to the woods that way.

He walked casually out towards the apple tree as if counting green apples, then just a little farther till he was half-hidden by a privet hedge. When he was completely hidden, he breathed easily again and felt suddenly free as he'd never felt before. No one knew where he was. He had maybe an hour before anyone would miss him, unless it was Rita. She wouldn't say anything; she'd just fuss at him when he got back.

He was trying to get through the thick growth around the old pigpen so he could start up the side of the hill. A thorny haw bush slapped him in the face, brambles grabbed at his feet, his hair even got caught in one bush as he crawled under it. He tasted blood on his lip where the thorns had scratched him, and he wiped his face on his sleeve.

Finally he was climbing the side of the hill which was steeper than it was right behind the house. He was glad he hadn't taken a second piece of cake as he realized how much easier it was to climb since he'd lost weight. It hadn't been easy to turn down desserts, especially ice cream and cake. But it was really worth it, and Daddy had promised him a dollar for each pound he lost. That meant about five dollars already!

He was almost to the top of the hill. He caught hold of a sweet shrub and stopped to breathe a minute. He heard a rustling in the leaves below him. Footsteps! Who . . . ? Surely the camper wouldn't be this close to the house! Maybe he was spying around to see if he could rob them while Daddy wasn't there.

He saw a glimpse of blue through the bushes and then Rita came into plain sight. He slid to his seat and waited for her, relieved and yet irritated.

"You didn't tell me you were going to sneak off," said Rita panting as she sat down beside him.

"Maybe I didn't want you to come," he said bluntly.

"Why not?"

"Because . . . I don't have to have any reason."

"Where are you going anyway?"

"Nosey! Why don't you go back to the house? I won't be gone long. Please, Rita."

"You're going to climb the queen tree and see if you see smoke again, aren't you?"

"How did you know?"

"Because I saw it, too. Do you think someone might have a still or something?"

"A still! What makes you think it's a still?"

"Well, I saw a movie once about a sheriff finding a still where they make whiskey. And that's how he found it. By going over in a helicopter and seeing the smoke."

"I hadn't thought about that," Frank said.

"We better go if we're going. Mama will miss us when the people all leave."

"Oh, OK. Let's go." Frank was really glad she had come, but it wouldn't do just now to let her know it.

The sunshine made long golden bars of light between the heavy tree shadows. Their steps sounded loud in the leaves since there was hardly any other sound. They stopped to eat a few late huckleberries and then trudged on.

When they reached the king and queen trees, Frank climbed up quickly to take a look. The wind lifted his hair deliciously as he looked out over the tiny valley. The late afternoon sun gave everything a purplish tinge. Away in the distance a water tower gleamed. A road cut whitely through the thick foliage, a tiny string of a road that appeared and disappeared going into Stanton.

"I don't see any smoke," he called down. "Not a bit."

"Then come on down. It's lonesome down here," Rita said. And as Frank came down she added, "I guess we better go back home, huh?"

"No. I'm going to see the brook again."

"Well. But it is so spooky quiet. It wasn't like this before."

"No. David Oliver and Shelley were with us. You're not scared, are you?"

"No, of course not! It's just spooky."

The brook was singing a little song as it rushed over stones and around jutting tree roots. One giant root made a bridge across the stream. Frank was walking across it when a wild Indian yell chilled his blood. He stood frozen, arms outstretched for balance. Rita was wading, making little dams with her feet when the noise came. Her hands flew to her ears, and she looked quickly in every direction. "What was that?" she screamed. She had hardly gotten the words out when the noise came again, more terrifying than before.

"Who's there?" demanded Frank in what seemed to him a very weak, scared voice. There was no answer, but there was a presence nearby. They could feel it. Someone was trying to scare them away, and suddenly it made Frank angry. "This is my aunt's land and it may be ours soon," he called out. "You'd better identify yourself or I'm going to call the sheriff."

There was no answer.

"Gee, Frank, you sound really mean," said Rita in a loud respectful whisper.

"You have to if . . . ." He didn't get to finish his sentence, for suddenly a wild-looking man was walking toward them through the bushes. His long hair was bushing out around his head; his teeth were bared like an animal's.

Rita stumbled through the water getting to the root to be close to her brother. The hideous

creature was standing on the bank just looking
at them as if they were nice specimens for a
collection.

"You kids run on home," he said gruffly, but
somehow they couldn't budge. He looked like a
half-breed Indian with high cheekbones, some
dark paint smudged on the tops of his cheeks, and
very dark hair. But he had a beard which didn't
look like the Indians in the movies and his bare
chest was hairy. Maybe Indians were hairy, but
they never appeared so.

"I said go home," he repeated, and shook a
heavy stick at them.

"I think *you* should go home," said Frank,
walking boldly towards him.

"Frank, don't get near him," cried Rita, but
Frank kept wading.

"You think you're smart, don't you, kid," the
man said, but he didn't move from where he stood.

As Frank got closer, his heart thudding, he saw
that the man's upper lip was jerking in a nervous
twitch. He really didn't look very old either,
maybe twenty, but not old. Frank started to climb
the mossy bank, but the man stepped back and
held both hands out as if to say "Don't touch me."

"I'm going to have to tell my father about you,"
said Frank solidly, beginning to feel sorry for the
person. He saw that the paint on his cheeks was
mud from the brook, smeared and slapped on
hastily.

"No! You can't tell anyone about me! Listen,

kid," the man said, calming himself by putting one hand in a pocket of his muddy pants. "Listen," he repeated, "I've never hurt you, have I?"

"No."

"Well, I never meant to and I never will. So please don't hurt me by telling. Promise?"

"But . . . what are you doing in my Daddy's woods?"

The man leaned against a tulip tree and then slid down to a sitting position. Picking up a dried leaf, he began to break it into small pieces. Rita had come closer now, too, and stood just behind and to one side of Frank, drying her feet on a tuft of moss.

"You are nice kids. So I hate to tell you what I'm about to tell you. But you might as well know. Maybe, if you know, you'll be kind enough not to tattle on me."

"I don't know," said Frank hesitantly.

"Well, anyway, there's a cabin just down the stream," he said nodding his head in that direction. "It's kind of hidden in the laurel bushes so you might not have ever seen it. I've been there for oh, three weeks, I guess."

"Then it was you we heard walking over here before," said Rita.

"Yeah. I hoped you wouldn't come back."

"What have you done?" demanded Frank boldly.

"I . . . well, I ran away from a reform school. I wasn't supposed to be there anyway really. I'd gotten in with a bad crowd, but I never broke into that filling station myself." All the time he was talking he kept glancing up and then looking again at the leaf he was tearing up.

"You didn't help with a robbery?" asked Rita hopefully.

"No. I wouldn't go with them that night. But they were mad at me so when they got caught they said I'd helped them plan it."

"And you didn't?"

"No! I didn't!" he said sharply, throwing the last bit of leaf to the ground. "I tell you I didn't have anything to do with it. And you have no idea how mean they can be at a reform school until you've gone there yourself. The other kids, I mean. Everybody hates everybody. It's awful!" He dabbed at his eyes and tears mixed with mud came off on his hand.

"Well, gee, that's terrible," said Frank in awe. "Where's your mom and dad?"

"They don't believe me either. Especially my Mom. She hates me like everybody else." There was a sob in his voice.

"Your Mom hates you?" asked Rita.

"Yeah, but listen now, do you kids promise not to tell? See, I won't be here much longer. It was night when I got here and I fell over a log and sprained my ankle. But it'll be well soon and I'll get out of your woods. You won't tell, will you?"

Frank looked down at the man's swollen foot with no shoe on and realized why he was carrying the big stick and why he'd sat down so quickly. Frank looked at Rita and then back to the man with his grubby beard and hairy chest. Was it right to help this man even in such a little way? After all, Daddy had said before that if you help a criminal, you're becoming one yourself. And yet the Bible said, "Love your neighbor as yourself." And surely this man was a neighbor.

"What's your name?" he asked.

The man hesitated just a second as if maybe he weren't sure he could tell. "Lester," he said then. "Lester Johns."

"Well, gee, Mr. Johns. . . ."

"Oh, you can call me Lester. I'm really not very old you know, just seventeen."

"But you've got so much beard!" exclaimed Rita.

Lester grinned. "Yeah. But I'm telling the truth. You don't have to believe me, but I was seventeen in January."

"Oh. Well, sure, we believe you."

"And now will you promise?" he asked again, looking up at them with pleading eyes.

"But, sir, I mean, Lester, see, my Daddy's a doctor and maybe he could help you get all this straightened out. I know he'd try real hard. He always worries about people who have problems. I know he would want to help you."

"He couldn't help me! No one can! I've just got to get away, that's all!" He beat his fist against his forehead and his eyes were wet when he looked up again. Very carefully, as if he were starting all over again with his explanation he began, "Now, listen, kids, I'm in trouble. I've never hurt you, and I'd help you in any way that I could if I found you in trouble anywhere. Please do me this one favor. Please."

Frank swallowed as he tried to decide which was the worse thing to do, turn the man in when he seemed so in need of getting away, or just not say anything. "OK," he said slowly, "I promise. I promise not to tell."

"And you, little girl?" asked Lester, looking at Rita hopefully.

"Yes. My name is Rita Patterson and I promise not to tell," she said solemnly.

"Oh, and my name's Frank. And uh, I guess we better get going. Our Mom doesn't like for us to be so far from the house. Uh, will you be all right?"

"Sure," Lester laughed. "If I've made it this long surely I can make it a little longer. Of course, some leftover food sure would taste good."

"Oh, yeah. I guess it would. We'll see what we can do. But we've got to go now."

They ran back across the brook and waved from the other side before they were hidden from sight among the laurel bushes.

5

The first time Frank took food to Lester it was easy. He wasn't gone long and his mother never even missed him. But the next time he had trouble.

Mrs. Patterson bought a bushel of peaches off a truck parked at Mrs. Rath's store. All the children were put to work washing, sorting, peeling, and cutting. They sat out on the porch in a circle with a big cooking pot in the middle for the cut peaches. Shelley and David Oliver had to empty peelings and keep everyone's bowl full of washed peaches.

The peaches took all day. There was no chance for Frank to leave. Late in the afternoon Mrs. Patterson was still canning, her face red with the heat.

"Mama, can't we just keep the rest to eat?" called Frank hopefully.

"No, we'll get some more just to eat. I want these to give to our friends in Atlanta and have some this winter for pies."

"What are we having for supper?"

"Oh, we'll just have hamburgers this time. I haven't time to cook much."

Frank's heart sank. He wouldn't have much to take Lester even if he could go. But he had to take him something. Lester had been so hungry he ate like a stray dog, even licking his plate. He said he'd been living on nuts and roots and berries. Frank wondered that he hadn't poisoned himself with some of them.

When everyone was in bed that night, Frank lay in his hot upstairs room thinking. Was it too late to take something to Lester? Would he ever be able to find the hidden cabin in the dark? He rolled over and told himself Lester could wait until tomorrow, but a picture of Lester's scraggly bearded face floated before him. His eyes even looked hungry!

Frank slipped out of bed, put on his jeans, and carrying his shoes, crept down the stairs. He tried to walk very lightly, but each step seemed to cause a terrible creak in the old boards. He stood still at the bottom, but he didn't hear any stir from Mama's room.

In the kitchen he got all the leftover hamburgers, hoping Mama would forget there'd been any. The moonlight was bright enough through the window so that he didn't turn on a light, but he had to fumble to get the bolt pulled back on the door. He sat on the porch steps to put on his shoes.

Finally he was climbing the hill behind the house. The moon looked as if it were running to keep ahead of a bank of gray clouds. Just as he went into the woods the clouds caught up with the moon and there was darkness. A roaring wind began to blow.

Frank had only been to the cabin once and that was in the daytime. Now with the moon shining only now and then it was very hard to see where he was going. As he came down the hill towards the brook, he began to whistle softly, hoping Lester would hear him.

The sound of the water was getting louder the closer he came to it. Suddenly he stumbled over a log and the hamburgers shot out of his hands. Luckily he had wrapped them well and they didn't get dirty, just mashed.

"Lester!" he called softly and then again louder. His heart was beating very fast. This was a wrong thing he was doing, and he really wondered why he had come.

He stood still on the edge of the thick laurel bushes that grew all along the brook. The moonlight shone whitely on the glossy leaves. Something slithery went down the bank and into the water. He shuddered and turned to go home, just as he heard footsteps behind him. Then there was a hand on his shoulder and he spun around to face Lester.

"What are you leaving for? You're not afraid of me, are you?" laughed Lester. "Since you're brave enough to come over here in the night like this, you wouldn't be afraid, would you?"

"Why, no. No, of course not," stammered Frank,

knowing Lester was making fun of him. "Here. Here's some hamburgers for you."

"Oh, thanks! Boy! Hamburgers! I haven't had one in *ages!* Come on down to the cabin."

"Isn't it awful dark down there?"

"You get used to it. And I could build a fire. Come on."

"No. I better go on. I sneaked out of bed. I better get back."

"Well, OK. But can you come again?"

"Maybe. I'll see."

"Frank," said Lester, reaching out and holding onto his arm. He was about to say something very important. Then his hand dropped and he just said, "Thanks." He hobbled back into the bushes and Frank heard his steps in the leaves as he went downstream to the hidden cabin.

The wind got louder and stronger as Frank started home. The moon was completely covered with clouds now and it didn't ever come out to help him see. He heard raindrops in the trees. A flash of lightning gave him an instant view of the ghostly tree trunks. He began to run.

He was out of breath when he got to the king and queen pines, but it was pouring down rain and the thunder was deafening. He must keep going. He walked, ran, and stumbled down the hill, across the wide sandy gully, up past the oak tree, and finally out to the edge of the woods.

As he went down the open slope towards the house, his legs were so weak that they gave way under him and he fell. The rain felt like a waterfall pouring on him, a cold waterfall. A flash of lightning followed by a loud crash of thunder and a powerful gust of wind made him struggle to his feet again.

He sloshed across the porch floor, took his shoes off, and eagerly reached to turn the door knob. It turned. But the door wouldn't open. He pulled harder. The bolt had been locked back. Mama must have gotten up and found it undone. Did she know he was gone? He stood there dripping, wondering what to do.

Then he remembered how David Oliver had worried Mama by climbing out his window, down the porch roof, and then down the maple tree. He worked his feet back into his soggy shoes and went around to David Oliver's window.

It was very hard climbing the tree since he was so slippery and he felt even heavier than usual. But he did manage to get to a limb where he could pull himself up over the edge of the tin porch roof. He decided against going in David Oliver's window. David Oliver might wake up and ask a lot of questions. He got down on his hands and knees and began crawling towards his own window at the front of the house.

The rain ran down his neck and chilled his backbone. The tin was slippery under him. Several times he slid towards the edge, but caught himself. A big limb of a nearby pine tree fell with a crash. The sound was terrifying. He tried to go faster, but it was hard with the wind blowing so hard.

At last he was prying open the screen of his own window and then crawling in. He stood there shivering and dripping and feeling thankful to be back in his cozy room. He set his shoes carefully on the floor and was about to pull off his jeans when, even with the wind so loud outside, he heard footsteps on the stairs.

He didn't know how he got in the bed so fast. But there he lay, the covers pulled up over his wet hair, his breathing coming fast and hard. The door opened.

"Frank," Mama said softly. "You all right?"

He lay very still hoping she wouldn't turn her flashlight where she could see all the water on the floor. She stood there for a long minute, then she closed the door and went across to Rita's room. He listened until she was all the way down the stairs before he began changing clothes.

6

Frank went to see Lester often during the next two weeks. Sometimes Rita went too, if they thought they could get by with it. David Oliver begged to go with them, but if he went they never went all the way to the brook. They only went to the top of the second hill where the king and queen pines stood. If David Oliver or Shelley found out about Lester, it would be just like telling Mama.

Lester taught them how to catch water lizards and then let them wiggle out between their fingers into the water again. He showed them how to make a whistle from a soft young sourwood sprout. He showed them the little round dug-out spring in the side of the hill. "And would you like a cup to drink from? Then, behold!" he said, folding a large oak leaf around itself in a cone shape and fastening it with a little stick.

It was always shadowy at the little cabin even when the sun was high. Sunshine came through in spots, making quivering circles as the wind stirred the laurel bushes. There was a rich ferny taste to the air.

"How's your foot, Lester?" Frank asked one Friday afternoon.

"Oh, it's better. Lots better. Fact is, I'll be leaving in a couple of days probably."

"Gee! Already? We're gonna miss you!"

"You really mean that, don't you?" said Lester, looking up from a piece of wood he was whittling.

"Sure I mean it. You're one of the neatest friends I've ever had."

"Wow! My Mom would sure be shocked to hear you say that. Oh, boy, you'd be whipped if anyone found out you were talking to me."

"Well, look, you're not so bad, Lester. I mean everyone makes mistakes and you just gotta say you're sorry and start over."

"It's not that simple, though. Not that simple."

"Yeah, well, I will miss you. Reckon you could send me a letter sometime?"

"No. You'd be best just to forget all about me."

"But I'm not going to," declared Frank stubbornly.

"You'd better. I have a way of messing up people's lives," he said gloomily, tossing the piece of wood down.

"Lester!" exclaimed Frank picking it up. "You've almost made a boat here. It looks just like one except for not being hollow. Can't you finish it?"

"Oh, sure, if you want. I'll give it to you for a going-away present. Maybe one for Rita too."

"Would you? Gee, thanks, Lester. I'll be back tomorrow. Maybe you'll have it finished then."

"Maybe. You better run now. I don't want to get you in trouble. Or me, either."

"OK. Bye, Lester," he said.

"Bye, Kid."

He looked back from just up the stream and couldn't see the cabin or Lester. They were really well hidden.

As he came down the hill towards the house, he broke into a run, delighting in how fast he could go. Dad's car was there. It was early for him to be home, and Frank couldn't wait to see him. He wished he could tell him about Lester. Maybe he could help Lester not to have to run away. But, of course, he'd promised not to tell and he wouldn't.

Dad was talking to Mama while she cooked supper, tipping his chair back against the wall and rocking lightly on the back legs. He jumped when Frank came in and reeled backwards in mock disbelief.

"Frank the Fatty is no more!" he exclaimed and then held out his hand. "Let me shake hands with a man who has the willpower to give up desserts."

Frank glowed inside, but tried not to show it. "Aw, Dad, gee whiz." he said.

"Daddy, Daddy," said Shelley running in from the den. "I've got some things to show you. See, I made this picture for you. That's you and Mommy and that's Frank up in the ladder tree and there's Rita and David Oliver and here's me in my swing you made me."

"My, my, what an artist you are!" exclaimed Daddy, mussing up her tumbled curls. "But what's this ladder tree?"

"Oh, it's just over in the woods a way," said Frank. "There are two tall pines on top of a hill and I wanted to climb one. So I nailed boards up the trunk. Dad, it's beautiful from up there!"

"But he won't let me go up," said David Oliver resentfully. "He thinks he's so big and smart."

"Now, now, David Oliver," said Mama, setting a dish of butter beans on the table. "Is that where you go so much, Frank?"

"Well, yes, ma'am, sort of."

"Sort of?" asked Dad, raising his eyebrows.

"Yes, sir. You should climb up there, Dad. You'd really love it!"

"I just might do that. I think I remember the trees."

"You can see all the way to Stanton," said Rita.

"You mean *you've* been up there, too?" asked Mama in shocked surprise.

"Yes, Mama. It wasn't hard."

"Now, really, Rita, you just mustn't . . . ."

"Mother, Mother," said Dad, holding up one hand. "Let's go see it before we pass judgment. We'll go in the morning. Hey, how about a picnic lunch?"

"Oh, can we, Mama, can we?" yelled all the children, all except Frank who was worried about how he would see Lester if everyone else were around.

"OK," said Mama smiling. "We'll have a picnic!"

7

That Saturday was one of those hot early August days when the cool of the trees feels so good. There was a haze over the mountains so that it was hard to be sure what was mountains and what was clouds in the gray-blue distance. The grassy field behind the house was thick with daisies. But the morning was so still that it seemed not a one was nodding. Only a butterfly, air-dancing, made any movement on the slope as the Pattersons started up it.

It was about 11:00 when they got to the king and queen pines. Dad went up at once and shouted down that it was really beautiful, even though it was so hazy. "You must come up, Martha," he called. "You could feel like a bird up here."

"No, thanks," she laughed as she spread out a towel to sit down on. "I'd rather be a quail or something that stays close to the ground."

Frank thought it was a good sign that she could laugh on her first adventure in the woods. He so hoped that Lester wouldn't build a fire or make any noise today.

The children were satisfied to play on top of

the hill for awhile. They buried each other in the deep leaves, played Indians and cowboys, and put on a circus, complete with clowns, a walking bear (David Oliver), and a ballet dancer (Rita). But after lunch Shelley and David Oliver began begging to go to the brook. Rita and Frank had tried to bribe them ahead of time not to mention the brook. But the bribe had not been big enough.

"Yes, that's a good idea. I've been wanting to walk down there myself," said Dad.

So to the brook they went, with Rita and Frank hoping that Lester would stay quietly in his cabin and that Dad wouldn't remember about the cabin if he knew about it. Frank knew that Dad had walked all over the place when he'd come up to sign papers back in March. But maybe he hadn't seen the cabin.

Frank and Rita guided the two small ones to wade upstream instead of down. They built a dam with Dad wading in to help. "We built dams like this when I was little," he said. "The trick is to work very fast, use a lot of stones and a lot of mud."

"But, John," worried Mama from the bank. "You're sticking your hands in where you can't see. You're going to get hold of a snake!"

"No, no. If I did, I'd let go of it in a hurry!" he exclaimed.

Shelley persuaded Mama just to dip her feet in the water as she sat on the bank. She squealed at the iciness of the water, but to please Shelley she willed her feet to stay in the water until they felt almost numb.

"Isn't it fun, Mama?" asked Shelley. And Mama agreed, but with very little enthusiasm.

They succeeded in getting quite a little pond behind their dam. They enjoyed it for awhile and then screamed with delight as Frank knocked a hole in the middle of the dam and let the water gush through.

Mama loved the soft moss and the tiny wildflowers. "I wonder if I could transplant them," she said.

"You won't need to do that, darling. You can come back and see them here anytime," said John, grinning at her from where he had dropped beside her.

She looked at him thoughtfully and smiled. "Just the same, I think I'll try making a terrarium with some of these precious little things. Shelley, get me some of those pretty little stones out of the brook, please."

"Oh, I've got lots of those at home, Mama," said Shelley.

"You mean you children have been here often?"

"Well, not really often, Mama," said Shelley, realizing she'd goofed.

"Martha," said John as he propped on one elbow and looked up at her. "Don't you think you could trust them a little?"

Mama looked as hurt as if someone had slapped her. "Don't you even care that they might be bitten or fall in an old well or something horrible?" she asked.

"Yes, of course I care. But look how much beauty and fun they'd miss if they didn't take any risks. But listen to me, Shelley," he said, realizing the little girl was still standing taking in every word, "If your Mama says not to come here without someone big, then you don't come. I'll have to punish you if you disobey."

"Then maybe you better punish Fr . . . ."

Just at that moment Rita grabbed Shelley by the hand and said, "Shelley, Shelley, come see the bird's nest. I just found it. It's got birdies in it!"

Soon after that Dad said they had to go. He had an appointment to talk with Dr. Guy.

"What about, Dad?" asked Frank eagerly.

"Just doctor talk," he said in the tone of voice that told them nothing.

"It really is a beautiful place," Mama said as they left. "Even the dark places," she added.

After Dad left to go to Stanton, Frank began wondering how he was going to get back over to see Lester. He was really glad when he heard the crunch of tires in the driveway. Company! Now maybe he could slip away.

It was Mrs. Clayton and Mrs. Rath. Little Chris Clayton had her cousin Michael with her so there was someone for Shelley and David Oliver to play with. Rita was busy fixing her mother's terrarium, having no idea that Frank was going adventuring today. After being very polite to the ladies, Frank

drifted around the corner of the house and soon was gone.

As he got near the cabin, panting because he had run half the way, Frank wondered what Lester had thought about all the noise they had made. He grinned as he thought how close Lester had come to being found out and how he and Rita had worked 'to keep him safe.

"Lester!" he called out, stopping by a sourwood to catch his breath. "It's just me, Lester!" he yelled.

There was no answer. Quickly he stumbled through the bushes and jumped across the brook. "Lester! It's me," he shouted. "Lester!"

He stood at the doorway of the cabin a minute, letting his eyes adjust to the dark inside. "Lester? Lester!" he cried. Then kneeling beside him, "What's wrong?"

8

Lester groaned and turned fitfully. "I'll be OK soon. Don't tell anyone I'm here," he begged. "Just get me some water and leave me alone."

Frank ran to fill the canteen at the spring. His heart thudded in a fear he hadn't felt since the day he thought Shelley was snakebitten. If only Lester would let him tell Dad!

"What hurts, Lester?" asked Frank after he'd given him some water.

"It's my stomach. It hurts so bad," he said and then gritted his teeth in pain.

Frank laid a hand on Lester's forehead and against his cheeks as he'd seen his mother do. "You're hot," he said. "You're real hot."

"I know. But I'll be OK. Just go on and let me be sick in peace. Just as soon as I'm able I'll get off your land." He held his stomach and rolled in pain.

"You don't have to go, Lester. You can't run all your life, can you?"

"If that's what it takes."

"But, Lester. . ."

"Get out!" he screamed, getting up on his knees

and waving towards the door. "Go on! I don't want
you fussing over me. Just go!"

Frank stood at the door wondering what to do.
Lester was terribly sick. He needed a doctor. But
Frank had promised not to tell. Suddenly he
backed out the door as the sick man grabbed his
walking stick and lunged at him.

He ran across the brook and from the other side
saw Lester crumple, bending double with pain,
and fall back into his corner. The stick fell across
the log doorstep, balanced there for a minute, then
slid out the door, rolling a few inches before it
hung up on a laurel sprout. Frank stepped back
across the brook to give it back to Lester before
he left. Picking it up, he stood a minute looking
at all the names Lester had carved along its sides
as he waited in the little dark glen.

There were Rita's and his amongst all the other
names that he didn't recognize. He felt honored
that Lester had carved their names too, and
wondered what all those other people were like.
How could Lester leave everyone like that and
never see them again? But, of course, he probably
didn't see them much anyway in reform school.

He stood the stick quietly inside the door and
started to slip off as Lester seemed to be asleep.
But then he spoke in a pained quivering voice,
"I'm sorry, Frank. Best friend I ever had. Didn't
mean to hurt you. Hurt enough already. No one
understands. Didn't mean to, didn't mean to!" His
voice was rising to a high desperate pitch.

Frank knelt beside him again and held onto his hands that groped for something to hold. "I know you didn't mean it," he said. "You're just hurting so bad." He paused a minute listening to Lester's quick, shallow breathing. "Lester," he said then, "do you believe in God?"

"I don't know. Used to. Anymore . . . don't know."

"Well, I do. And I'm going to pray for you all the way home. You hear me, Lester?"

"Yeah. But, Kid, whatever you do, don't tell anyone that I'm here. I can't go back there. Can't!"

Frank smoothed the hair from his forehead and looked into the pained brown eyes. "I won't," he said.

He ran all the way home, stopping now and then to catch his breath and say a prayer for Lester. He still didn't know what to do. But he was really wondering now just how far you have to go in keeping a promise? What if it really hurts the one you promised? Then what?

As he approached the house he saw that a strange car was there. And Dad was back which meant Frank had been gone much longer than he'd realized. He wiped sweat on his shirt sleeves and squinted at the sun in the west. Must be nearly 6:00.

"Frank! Where have you been?" exclaimed his mother at the door. "And why have you been running so? Did something scare you?"

"No, ma'am. But I need some water."

He tried to ignore the hurt look in her eyes. He used to tell her everything that happened. But now he just couldn't always. Especially this.

"We have company," she said as he finished a whole glass of water. "The Dickersons."

"The Dickersons! That boy's folks?"

"Yes. They're going out on their own searching now. The FBI is about to give up. They'd like to ask you a few questions."

"Me? Why me?"

"They've already talked to us. Come on out on the front porch."

This was no time to be worrying about the Dickerson boy with Lester lying over there sick. But what could he do?

Rita was sitting on the porch rail kicking a foot against one post. She glanced at Frank when he came out and then looked down, studying the buttons on the front of her blouse. David Oliver and Shelley were playing Chinese checkers and arguing about who could jump where. Dad was in the swing and Mama sat down beside him as she said, "Frank, this is Mr. and Mrs. Dickerson."

Just for a minute he thought he'd seen Mr. Dickerson before. But he knew he hadn't. He wiped his hands on his jeans before shaking Mr. Dickerson's outstretched hand.

Mrs. Dickerson held a handkerchief tightly in one hand. "Ask him, Honey," she said almost impatiently.

"OK. Frank, our boy's been gone for about six

weeks and the FBI have checked possible contacts all over the country. They're about to give up. But what we're wondering is, maybe he didn't go so far. He didn't have any money. So . . ."

"Well, your Mama says you're in the woods a lot," said Mrs. Dickerson.

"And we thought you might have seen him," finished Mr. Dickerson sitting back down in the straw-bottomed chair.

"Have you, Frank?" asked Mrs. Dickerson with painful eagerness in her voice.

Frank remembered the bits of information on this woman, how she'd made her husband's boy so unhappy, especially after that awful accident. Even if he had seen the boy he wasn't sure he would tell, just the way he didn't know now what to tell about Lester.

"No, ma'am, I haven't seen him," said Frank.

"Oh, but show him the picture, Jim," said Mrs. Dickerson quickly as if she weren't ready for another no. "We've been going to all the neighbors, Frank, just hoping someone will have seen him."

"Why didn't you do that sooner?" asked Frank boldly.

"Frank!" said Dad sharply. "Just look at the picture and tell the truth if you've seen the boy."

"No, no, let me explain," said Mrs. Dickerson, dabbing at new tears. "See, Frank, my husband did look all along in places he thought Kevin might have gone. But I didn't. I didn't want Kevin back.

He had shot my little girl and I—I hated him."

"Sara, please. . . ," said her husband, putting a hand on her shoulder.

"No, I've got to," she sobbed. "I've got to make somebody believe!"

Frank swallowed and realized his knees were shaking from running so hard and being afraid for Lester and now something else.

"Frank, I was terribly, terribly wrong and I hurt Kevin so badly that I wouldn't blame him if he never came back. See, I took his father, he thought, and then I just shoved him out of everything I could. And—and I'm sorry. I really want him back. I want to try to make it up to him somehow."

Mr. Dickerson was still holding the wallet-size picture and he handed it now to Frank. It was of a clean-shaven handsome young face. Again there was something familiar, something nagging at Frank's brain. Had he seen him at the store or something?

"Of course Kevin was only fourteen there. He's seventeen now, but that's the latest picture we have," said Mr. Dickerson, clearing his throat uncomfortably. "Have you seen him?"

"No, sir, I don't think so."

"Are you sure?"

"Yes. Yes, sir, I'm sure," said Frank handing it back.

"Well, I guess we may as well go then," he said, standing up, a gray look of defeat across his long face. "Come on, Sara, we've taken up enough of their time."

"But you mustn't go without some iced tea or something," said Mrs. Patterson jumping up. "Please sit back down, and I'll bring it to you."

"No. No, we can't. Thank you, though. You've been very kind. We'll never forget."

9

It seemed forever before Frank could catch Dad alone. Then it was out at the tool shed where his father was rummaging curiously among Aunt Minnie's great variety of junk and old tools.

"Dad, I need to talk," said Frank.

"Sure, Son. What is it?" asked Dad as he looked at a hand-cranked ax sharpener. "This must have been Grandad's. Aunt Minnie got a lot of his things."

Frank couldn't think how to start. Lester might not be there anymore. He might have gotten better and left. But what if he were dying?

"Dad," he said quickly, not allowing himself to change his mind. "There is a man over in the woods and he's real sick."

Dad looked at him sharply and left the ax grinder, stepping towards him out of the cobwebby duskiness of the shed.

"And it's not Kevin Dickerson?"

"Why, no, of course not, Dad. His name's Lester Johns. He's been there for awhile. See, he ran away from a reform school. He didn't really steal the way they said, and he said people were real mean to him at that school."

Dad's eyes seemed to flash behind his glasses in the near darkness. Frank squirmed. "You've been seeing this boy all summer, Frank?"

"Yes, Sir, almost," he mumbled, his head down.

"And I trusted you!"

"But, Dad, Rita and I promised we wouldn't tell. We felt so sorry for him. He had a sprained ankle and he's real nice. Only now he's awful sick. Dad, you've got to look at him. I had to tell you. Breaking a promise would be better than letting him die." He sobbed as Dad put an arm around him.

"It's OK, Son. You've done right to tell. He's sick, and we'll have to help him. Your mother knows nothing of this?"

"Oh, no, I told you, you're the first one. Only Rita knows."

"Well, we're going to have to tell your mother now. Secrets are dangerous. It sure is a bad time for her to get news like this," he said, slamming the shed door shut. "Why couldn't it have been next month? But no, it's better as it is. It was too much to hope for anyway," he went on, talking to himself. Then they were climbing the porch steps. Frank didn't have time to ask him what he was talking about before they were going in the door.

"Martha," Dad called, "Frank has something to tell you."

"Well, can't he tell me while I fix supper?"

"No. I think you better come on the back porch. And hold up on supper. Frank and I'll be gone for awhile. I'm going to change clothes while you talk."

He held the screen for her to come out, stood a minute looking from one to the other, and then went inside. "Tell her everything, Frank. The whole thing."

Later Frank and his Dad approached the cabin and found Lester still groaning and smelling of sour vomit. Dad snapped open his black bag quickly and began taking Lester's temperature, looking in his eyes, listening to his heart, and taking his blood pressure. Even though Frank introduced his Dad, Lester seemed unaware that anyone was there. Dad said he was delirious and didn't know what was going on.

"I think he has appendicitis," said Dr. Patterson, rocking back on his heels. "We have to have a stretcher to get him out of here."

"How will we get one, Dad?" asked Frank, turning the flashlight off to save the batteries.

"We'll have to call the ambulance. One of us has to go back to the house. I only told Martha to call Dr. Guy. He won't know he needs to send the ambulance."

"Well, you go, Dad," said Frank. " 'Cause see, Lester knows me. If he should come to, it'd be better for me to be here."

"I guess you're right. OK. I'd better hurry then.

Think you can do without the flash?"

"Oh, yes, sir. I'll be OK."

Father and son were quiet in the darkness for a minute. There was the sound of the water rushing by outside and there in the corner Lester's hot, quick breathing and continuous moaning.

"I'll be OK, Dad," Frank said again.

Dad found his shoulder in the dark and grasped it firmly. "I believe you will. I'm proud of you, Son," he said as Frank handed him the flashlight.

Frank shivered in the darkness as he heard his dad's steps fade away beyond the rumble of the brook. A mosquito bit him on the ear and another on his hand. His slaps sounded loud to him, but he heard no change in the moaning, fitful tossing of Lester. Lester said he wasn't sure he believed in God. If he didn't and he died right here this night—then where would he go? Frank tried not to think about that.

The darkness became suffocating to Frank. He thought if he went outside he could at least get a glimpse of stars in the sky through the thick foliage. He thought about building a fire. He knew where Lester kept the wood and the matches. But he remembered Shelley's snake and decided not to feel around too much in the dark. The few stars that he could pick out by tilting his head all the way around would have to be all the light he had. Lester might have a flashlight in his things, he thought suddenly, and groped his way back in to feel around the walls. But if there were a flashlight, he couldn't find it and finally gave up.

"Dad! No! Don't come in! I might hurt you, too," yelled Lester suddenly. Frank ran to him.

"Your Dad's not here, Lester. Lie down. You'll hurt yourself."

"Who are you?" he asked, groping in the air to feel him.

Frank took his hand. "I'm Frank. Your friend. I'm staying with you because you're so sick. You've gotta lie down, Lester."

As Lester settled back down on his tumbled bedroll, Frank wondered what he could have meant— "I might hurt you, too," he'd said. Why would he be afraid of hurting someone? Oh, well, it was just a sick person's dream, probably didn't have anything to do with his real life.

Frank sat on the doorstep waiting. It seemed safer somehow. He wasn't really afraid of Lester, he told himself. But he couldn't forget how he looked coming towards him with that stick and then to hear all his crazy talking. What if he really had helped with that robbery? But no, he had believed him when he was well and he wouldn't turn against him now that he was sick. Only the doorstep did seem a better place to wait. There was nothing he could do for him anyway.

There was a splash in the water as some little creature jumped in. "Poor Mama," he thought. "I guess she'll always be afraid of the country. I wish she could enjoy it. I guess this will really ruin it for her for sure." He had so wished they could move up to Aunt Minnie's house to stay, not have to go back to the city.

Frank stood up quickly as he heard the roar of a motor. It had to be closer than the highway. It had to be! It was. He was sure of it. Was Lester going to be mad at him? Would he still be his friend when he found out Frank had broken his promise?

The motor stopped, probably on the second hill. Could they have gotten that far through the trees and over the gullies? Frank went to be with Lester as he waited. He tried to give him some water, but Lester wouldn't have it.

There were bright lights coming through the trees, shifting rhythmically with the walking of the men. There was mumbling talk between them and Frank picked out his Dad's voice from the rest.

Lester was hard to handle, but there were plenty of men and he was so weak now he couldn't fight much. Frank wasn't sure whether he knew what was happening to him or not. He walked along behind the stretcher with Dad. The lights played weird tricks with the shadows of the men, throwing them along the floor of the woods or partly on tree trunks and bushes, long skinny body shadows with stilt-like legs.

Dad arranged for Frank to ride in the ambulance with Lester since no one else knew him. He sat in front with the driver and another man. There were two men with Frank and Lester.

In all his life as a doctor's son Frank had never ridden in an ambulance before. It seemed so strange to ride past the house, which was all lit up, with the children, and Mama waving to them from the porch.

Then he heard Lester whispering something. The siren had just been turned on and he didn't hear what he said.

"What is it, Lester? I didn't hear."

"Whatever you hear," Lester said then, "whatever they tell you, I didn't mean to do it. She just ran in front of me. I couldn't stop." There was a sob in his voice which ended in a horrible shaking groan. The medical assistant moved over and held Lester on the stretcher with strong firm hands.

10

At the hospital Frank was suddenly not needed anymore. Dr. Guy had gotten there, and Dad assisted him in emergency surgery. They had disappeared through big swinging doors and left Frank standing helplessly in the long, gloomy hall. He ambled to the waiting room and leafed idly through a magazine. Then he looked around the small room. There was only room for about a dozen people to sit and wait. The only other person there was a man asleep, lying across three of the dark green plastic upholstered chairs.

When Dr. Guy and Dad came out, Frank rushed to them.

"How is he?" he asked eagerly.

"Fine. He'll be fine," said Dr. Guy. He held out his hand to Frank. When Frank gave him his hand, Dr. Guy covered it with his other hand.

"Frank," he said, "when did you first meet Lester?"

"Gosh, I don't know. It's been weeks."

"More than a month?"

"I guess. Maybe that."

"Come sit down, Frank. You, too, John.

"Frank, Lester's name is really Kevin Dickerson and you've probably saved his life in more ways than one. Just by being a friend to him when no one else was helped him. And there are a couple of people who will want to thank you, I know. Jim and Sara Dickerson."

The Dickersons! But Lester was Lester. He couldn't be Kevin Dickerson. Then Frank remembered how familiar Mr. Dickerson had looked and the picture of Kevin they had shown him.

"But how . . . he said he ran away from a reform . . ."

"Frank, he wouldn't want to tell you the truth for several reasons. He was running away from home and trying to run away from the awful thing he'd accidentally done. And, too, he wanted you to think well of him."

"You might say," said Dad, "that he was running away from himself."

"Oh." That was all Frank could think of to say. How dumb he had been! Some detective he would make!

"But, Dad," he said, suddenly grabbing his arm. "What about Mrs. Dickerson? Is she really going to be kind to him now? Dad, I'm not sure!"

"I am," said Dad firmly. "And anyway, it's not any of our business."

The Dickersons came through the door just then and came right to them. "How is he?" Mr. Dickerson asked anxiously.

"He's going to be just fine, Jim," said Dr. Guy. "We got him just in time, thanks to Frank here."

Mrs. Dickerson looked at Frank and seemed to read doubt in his eyes. "You didn't have to hide him," she said, "you could have told us. I am really different now, Frank, I won't be unkind to him anymore."

"But, I didn't know who he was," stammered Frank. He knew by the expressions on their faces they didn't believe him, but he didn't try to convince them. Somehow it just didn't matter.

"Thank you, Frank, from the bottom of my heart," said Mr. Dickerson, his face actually glowing even in the dull waiting room light.

Dr. Guy cleared his throat. "Our patient will be waking before long now. There's a coffee machine down the hall if you'd care for some while you wait."

"Oh, no, thanks. But, Doctor," Mrs. Dickerson said, twisting and untwisting her fingers, "do you think I'll be able to see Kevin tonight?"

Dr. Guy hesitated, then smiled and patted her on the shoulder. "Just for a minute, dear. And now I must be running. John, good to see you, and thanks a million for the help. Maybe things will work out for us soon. I'm counting on it," he said, as he shook his hand.

"Thanks, sir. I hope so, too."

"Dad, can't I see Lester tonight?" asked Frank.

Dr. Guy answered instead of Dad. "Not tonight,

Frank. I'll tell him you're coming tomorrow. How's that, huh?"

"Yes, Sir," he said in disappointment. It was hard to believe that the parents Lester had been so hurt by were the ones who would see him tonight and not he, who had really cared for him when he was down and out.

It was the next afternoon when Dad took Frank to see Lester. He was sitting up in bed looking quite pale and very strange with all his beard shaved off.

"Hey, Kid, this is really neat! Did you bring me some spring water?"

"No, Crazy. But you'll be back soon to get some yourself, you know."

"Yeah. Maybe so. That's a nice spring."

There was a strain between them. Lester was covering up more now than he had before. At least that's how it seemed. If this were the real Kevin, then Frank wished he could have stayed like Lester. He was so much easier to talk to.

"Uh, what happened to your beard?" he asked, waving a hand.

"I guess the hospital wanted to clean me up real good. Looks different, doesn't it?" he grinned as he rubbed his chin. "Great little hospital here. There aren't enough nurses to bug you all the time like they do some places." He rolled his bed up and down experimentally.

"Lester, I mean, Kevin . . ." began Frank

carefully. "Are you mad at me?"

"Now, Frank, old boy, how could I be mad at you? The doctor said you saved my life. By the way, we need to talk to my Dad about a reward for you."

"Oh, no, please!" exclaimed Frank, looking Lester in the eye. "It's just that . . . well, I'm sorry I broke my promise. But I had to."

There was silence in the little room with its gray-green furniture. Lester picked threads from one pajama sleeve. Finally he said, "It was too much to ask. You couldn't really believe that I'd rather die. It's OK, Frank. Don't worry. I'll make out."

Frank felt really dismal. He walked over to the window and looked out. There were squirrels playing in an oak tree.

"She says she's different and she wants me to forgive her," Lester said then. "But, well, it's just hard to forget all the things she's said before. I guess . . . I guess I'm glad to be alive, though. Really."

Frank was about to say something when the door burst open and Mr. Dickerson came in carrying a little girl dressed in a dainty pink pantsuit. "It's against regulations, but I got special permission," he said grinning.

The little girl squealed frantically, "Kevin! My Kevin! Oh, Kevin!" The whole upper half of her body was one wriggling mass of motion. Mr. Dickerson set her on the edge of the bed and she lay across Kevin's chest laughing and crying. His

arms closed around her as he let out a deep trembling sob. "Oh, Jenny!" he cried burying his face in her curls.

There were tears streaming down Mr. Dickerson's face as he watched the reunion. Frank started quietly for the door. But just as he pulled the door open, Lester called out in a choked voice, peering over Jenny's head, "Frank, don't forget your boat I carved for you. There's one for Rita, too. On a big stone behind the cabin. And Frank . . ."

"Yeah?"

"Thanks," he said, and grinned through his tears.

ɛ

11

August was almost over. Soon they would be going back to Atlanta. Frank had heard Daddy tell Mama only last weekend not to worry anymore about moving. Atlanta wasn't that far away, he said, so maybe they could come up for some holidays and he'd be happy. They could sell most of the land, just keep the house and yard for a holiday retreat.

Frank knew that any day now Mama would start them all to packing their things. He dreaded it so. Kevin had come one day after church and gone to the woods with him. He and Kevin understood each other, even though they weren't the same age. He would miss him and, most especially, he would miss the woods.

"Frank, come on, don't you want to wade any?" called Rita, standing on a mossy stone in the middle of the stream.

"No, I guess not," he said gloomily, tossing a pebble into a deep place and watching the ripples go out in circles.

"Frank, we're going back to Atlanta soon," said David Oliver. "You better play while you can."

"I'm just not in the mood."

Later as they walked home Rita tried to comfort her brother.

"We'll still be able to come up in the summers. And maybe Mama will decide it's not so bad after a year or two. I think she already likes it. Maybe we can move here to stay next year."

"But Dad's going to sell the land. I just want to move now and keep it all!"

"I know. Me, too."

They stopped in amazement at the top of the grassy slope behind the house. There was Dad's car and it was only Thursday. Dad never came on Thursday. Shelley and David Oliver ran ahead in excitement, but Frank and Rita held back.

"This is it, I guess," said Frank. "He's come to move us back. That's why he's early."

When they went in the house Shelley grabbed Rita by the hand and said, "Come see!"

As they followed her they almost fell over stacks of boxes in the middle of the floor. Frank felt sick. The packing had started.

In the living room there were more boxes, not as many. But what Shelley was pointing at was the windows. Instead of the old droopy green drapes Aunt Minnie had left on them, they were hung with new flowered drapes on shiny brass rods.

"Do you like the new drapes, Frank?" asked Mama, her eyes unusually bright.

"She made them herself, Frank!" said Shelley,

glad to be able to add that bit of information.

"But why, Mama?" asked Rita. "I mean they're as nice as the ones in Atlanta. They're beautiful!"

Daddy put his arm around Mama and held her tight. Frank felt pleased and embarrassed all at once the way he always did when Daddy hugged Mama. That's why he didn't hear at first what Daddy said and had to ask him to say it again.

"We're moving here to stay, Frank. I'll be working with Dr. Guy in Stanton."

"But, all the boxes?"

"I just brought them. They're my medical books."

"But you said last weekend . . . you said you'd sell the land."

"You didn't hear what I said, Frank," said Mama. "I said if he wanted to be a doctor here he should be a doctor here. You all can teach me not to be afraid. We can learn, can't we, Shelley?" she said as Shelley snuggled up against her.

"We're really going to live here?" asked Rita in wonder.

"We really are," said Mama and Daddy together, laughing with each other.

"Whoopee!" shouted Frank and David Oliver as the truth finally sank in.

"Turkey Hill House is home, it's really home!" shouted Frank and felt as if he would explode with happiness. In his joy he hugged everyone and danced like a little boy.

"I'm going to call Lester—I mean Kevin—and

tell him. Boy, is he ever going to be surprised!"

And so it was that the Pattersons became, not just the Pattersons *at* Turkey Hill House, but the Pattersons *of* Turkey Hill House.